Photonic Postcard

Pragya Suman

Ukiyoto Publishing

All global publishing rights are held by

Ukiyoto Publishing

Published in 2021

Content Copyright © **Pragya Suman**

ISBN 9789356970304

All rights reserved.
No part of this publication may be reproduced, transmitted, or stored in a retrieval system, in any form by any means, electronic, mechanical, photocopying, recording or otherwise, without the prior permission of the publisher.

The moral rights of the author have been asserted.

This is a work of fiction. Names, characters, businesses, places, events, locales, and incidents are either the products of the author's imagination or used in a fictitious manner. Any resemblance to actual persons, living or dead, or actual events is purely coincidental.

This book is sold subject to the condition that it shall not by way of trade or otherwise, be lent, resold, hired out or otherwise circulated, without the publisher's prior consent, in any form of binding or cover other than that in which it is published.

www.ukiyoto.com

Foreword

The Revelation is standing at the door.

Prose poetry, for some, is a form without a home, a form at the threshold of mutually exclusive modes of writing. It's a mongrel form, best kept separated from its pure-bred parents.

If this is the case, the prose poems gathered here in Pragya Suman's first collection amount to a whole litter of wild prodigies, scratching at the door, determined to be let in. They are endearing in their strangeness, yet the wildness in their eyes is a window to the uncomfortable uncanny. These are eyes which see right through you to *the whole stars of infinity*, before a single blink fixes them on the twitching energy in your skull and spine. Homeless, perhaps, but not lost; these are works which will dog your footprints and howl on the front step when you're trying to sleep.

Inevitably, sooner or later, you'll open the door a crack – you're only human, after all – and in they'll rush with their swords and crows, Hitler's moustache, their impossible juxtapositions, and bricks of butterflies tumbling out of nowhere. And all over those neat preconceptions about prose and poetry – not to mention those tidy categorisations of devine and degenerate – Suman's words are *leaving ... footprints in the strokes* of each startling image. *Owls are sipping cold coffee*, Van Gogh is waiting for his lover, and a close relative dies in the night.

After reading (and rereading) this collection, you may not be sure where you are or where you have been – this is what prose poetry does so well – but at your side you will have a dog made of butter. A mongrel? Maybe, but it will surely be more faithful than the gaudy show dogs of verse and narrative from which it came.

And what's that shadowy form scraping at the boundary?

Go and look!

Prof Oz Hardwick
Leeds Trinity University (UK)

Acknowledgement

This volume *Photonic Postcard* includes forty four prose poems written by me. Prose poetry is now highly significant and deserves critical attention. Initial twelve poems are ekphrastic prose poems written on a particular theme. I wrote them upon paintings of Vincent Van Ghogh, just as an experiment or prediction about the mood of Vincent at a time of creative process. Rest poems are on varied subjects, from personal to social. Some poems are shared by me on social media to get a response and judgement from people. They are not published in any magazine, print media or digital one.

About the Author

Dr Pragya Suman is a doctor by profession, from Bihar, India. She has done specialisation in ophthalmology and pathology. Writing is her passion which she inherited from her father. Her Father late Triveni prasad yadav was a civil engineer by profession who always kept his library up to date. Her mother was a housewife and a real motivator. Her husband Dr Bisheswar Kumar is also a doctor. She is the mother of a single daughter named Vatsalya. Her poetries, reviews and fiction have been published in many magazines and anthologies. She has achieved a certificate of excellence from many literary forums and Gujrat Sahitya Academy. Her poems are weekly broadcast from universal vision radio Mexico. She won the Gideon poetry award of summer 2020. Her favourite writers are Franz Kafka, WB Yeats, Robert Frost and David Thanne Cornell. She also writes short stories and reviews which have been published in many magazines and anthologies. Her debut book "Lost Mother" was published in 2020 and she is the Editor in Chief of Arc Magazine, India.

CONTENTS

Part 1 1
   Vincent And Autumn Landscape 2
   Vincent And Exercising Prisoners 3
   Vincent Is Peasant Painter 4
   Vincent In Thunderclouds 5
   Vincent In Forest 6
   Red Poppies Of Vincent 7
   Vincent And The Starry Night 8
   Vincent And Almond Blossom 9
   Vincent And The Potato Eaters 10
   Vincent's Shoe 11
   Vincent And Coffee Drinker 12
   Vincent And The Road Menders 13

Part 2 14
   Gregor Samsa Is Still Alive 15
   Marble Balls 16
   Coagulated City 17
   The Democratic Dungeon 18
   The Green Pond 19
   Fractured God 20
   Helium Balloon 21
   City Of Old Days 22
   Starfish 24
   Coins 25
   Riot 26
   Wine In The Coconut Shell 27
   Dungeon 28
   Olfaction 29
   The Black Soul 30

Balzac's Black Coffee	31
Golden Bird	32
Coins Of Corona	33
Bleeding Star	34
Fasting Farmers In The Supermarket	35
Part 3	36
My Father's Tunic	37
Alienated Laugh	38
Scandal	39
Inkwell	40
Coffer Box	41
Sharer	42
Bereavement	43
My Father's Wristwatch	44
Incarnation	45
Mother's Postcard	46
I Am Covid Positive	47
I Locked The Lake	48

Part 1

Vincent And Autumn Landscape

Autumn is at the door of Vincent and it seems his brush is running in a red river. Red dunes of Mars are heaped up in his horoscope and in a fiery mood he would commit suicide. Three tiny crows are wheeling in an ill omen and Vincent wants to hide in the purple sky. Soon his brush, bursting in grumpy grease would unmask him, as the sky is getting pale in patches and white wees in segmentation.

An artist sleeps in strikes off a matchbox and when he nudges fire lights up in the willows of three dimensions. The burnt bushes are going to make swindling trees into coagulated coal as Vincent and the stoic's scandal are twinning at the edges of red relics of pristine paint. One day his brush will engulf Vincent the lecherous.

That day, Violet Vincent would get bleached in white!

Vincent And Exercising Prisoners

The tallest walls have engulfed the sky and the condensed soul is encaged in a vertical cell, walls tolling above the tiny prisoners. Vincent is stultifying in the mental asylum, not of concrete brick, sand and soil, but of ethereal atoms which are parched and tossing in hot waves.

Two owls are fluttering in the cochlea of Vincent's ear as his soul is liquified in watercolour and oozing drop by drop in the dark ear. In medicinal words it is vertigo; in abstract words rotating soul. Prisoners are stooped, prisoners are upright: pale faces, dark faces, in a circle of guards.

A mysterious wheel is moving and a black hole is peeping through the window without a sill.

Till the owls are free, Vincent will paint in hell.

Vincent Is Peasant Painter

Vincent wants to tag himself nowadays as a peasant painter, just wants to paint them in a mellifluous mood but his masterstrokes betray him as some are strips upon wounds. Wisps of hair are drooping beneath the black bonnet of a woman because, beguiling, butterflies are fluttering in the stomach as procurers of the Netherlands are hungry. Black creek sheepishly emerges beneath the kneel of the nasal mountain, "puffing up sunken cheeks", but it seems Vincent has not gone berserk yet and, whenever he is tired, dark circles of tumuli begin to engulf him in the infinite sleep, and whole pains of peasants begin to pour out of the ocular prism. They only open when Vincent sleeps!

Vincent In Thunderclouds

One day when the neurons of a painter lost thick narcotic juice, a ball of thunderclouds began to descend vertically. Horizon is not semicircular but vertical on a wheatfield. Pale Vincent is hungry and seeking his lucid interval in green sheaves of wheatfield below the deepening azure sky.

I have heard black birds in Paris are gossiping.

A mad man is lost in the rectangle!

Vincent In Forest

I have seen vertical bars in the whistling wind and, as Vincent stalks among the grey birch, his black furs concoct with the breeze. Too much for poor Vincent! Alienation in solitary souls. Tall, decapitated trees have lost their sap and are grieved in grey. Even chopped ears turn grey, and one day Vincent will overcome the noisy wind with his deafness. Till then, Vincent will be blocked with his abstract soulmate among the surreal social distancing.

Nowadays Vincent is in the forest, beneath the black canopy, and white, green, pale leaves are weeping among the withering willows.

Red Poppies Of Vincent

Auvers is red and red, as red poppies are seekers of infinite sleep and petals are still in a closed fist. An Impressionist masterstroke splutters the infinite cerulean sky. One day petals will kiss a painter's brush.

When Vincent's fingers tighten, poppies' petals look lax.

Look! Green yews are gazing, the revelation is standing at the door.

Vincent And The Starry Night

Dark Cypresses are looming above. Soon they will puncture the sky, then dazzling Venus will give a white smile. Ethereal electrons in orbit are swirling waves of the mad man that have engulfed the whole stars of infinity. The tiny thatched houses with spiky minarets and their owners mock him and call him Madman. Soon Vincent will give them relief as hills are going to be crowned in his canopy.

He is awaiting the crescent moon to complete the cycle. Moonbeams are full of photons, which will pervade the skull of a mad man. Just peeping in the skull, a Milky Way is spread in the bottom and gamboling wavelets of a live ocean are percolating the bony chips. An Impressionist will soon arise to paint the dark soul.

The stark white soul is entering the astral world, the deep door of the moon.

Vincent And Almond Blossom

Solid spring is white, oozing out of the ringed branches, sprawling in Vincent's sky. An artist is twirling in a ring as the divine is hiding at the bottom of his spinal cord. The Impressionist is leaving his footprints in the strokes, dipping his brush in the oily liquid loch, in the gyri of glassy tumblers, while the ocean is colouring the divine canopy. Vincent has gone thick nowadays, making God blush in thin, transparent veils, as the battling brush has stroked away the dark dove.

Eternal energy swirling above the loin, up and up, is going to burst up the skull in a smooth surface, blooming upon the thick chimera. Almonds are agile in white fragrance. Serene, soft petals are sweet, though canvas has gone salty.

Vincent And The Potato Eaters

Vincent dipped his figurative fingers in the earthen bowl as they were sodden in sweat for years. Potatoes were stuffed in sunken cheeks and bulging eyes were sipping the black tea. In the canopy of pale bulbs, the Netherlands was dark and dark! The painter picked a single wrinkle, and nudged his star.

Vincent's ears are still stuck in the bowels of the potato eaters!

Vincent's Shoe

One day, Vincent was sleeping in the open courtyard as his money bag was perforated with many holes. A skylark swooped down and pecked his skull, making a gutter fracture. A thick soul, scooped out and sliced in half and half in two shoes, sat upon the vacant canvas. Vincent is nowadays in pale fibrous wrinkles; he plucks a pinch, to glue upon the paint. Shoes are now hard demons, battling upon the pale and russet rings. Demon's neck is worn out. Limpid thin divine soul has gotten rugged in war. A metamorphosis in thick shoes!

Two demons are looming on the horizon, clowning the stoic, and Vincent is still bargaining with the shoe-shopkeeper in the flea market.

Vincent And Coffee Drinker

Vincent has peeled off receptors nowadays, as Balzac comes to him in animated figures. Balzac coffee is still fresh and they are churned in painter's copper mugs. Vincent counts figures, though his eyes are prodding the flirting tail of a cat whose arrival is delayed.

You know coffee drinkers are flirters but an old man's cupid arrow is shrunken and he is in a dilemma.

He will play sorcery in the saucer and when the painter is a sleep, the old man will drink the whole coffee sheepishly.

Balzac was a flirt but Vincent is still waiting for his lover, who hid in the scintillating square smeared with coffee stains. But one day Vincent will seek her because he has got figurative nowadays and the whole ethereal snow is denuded and hot.

Checkered chessboards are going to breach soon, as white whiskers have promised crossed legs, and they will only weave smoky stories!

Vincent And The Road Menders

The pale wrinkled waves are leaping above the gigantic trunks and Vincent is wriggling in the courtyard of the mental asylum. It seems fire of the abyss, fire of heaven and fire of pyre are alighted in Vincent's soul, and he is beaming at berserk. Vincent uses watercolour, likes to reside at the rim between viscous and vibrant. Red bobs are calling from windows. Menders are trying to repair the mind amid the black-cloaked death. Stones and sands are strewn beside pavements in pestle green. Perhaps seed will erupt soon. The brain of the artist is fleshy and the mind is fiery, but Vincent will sleep soon, deep and deep in the ethereal lamppost.

Part 2

Gregor Samsa Is Still Alive

Gregor Samsa woke up one morning and saw himself transformed into a worm, though he left us along with "snot brake" moustache Hitler long years ago. But I saw him again in a bag of worms, wriggling, expelled out of the operated intestine.

[Surgical scalpels–operation table–intestinal obstruction]

I lifted him with forceps. He ballooned up in big bulk, perhaps air was sucked in the intestine of the kafka. I asked about his parched skin.

"I like to melt, bit by bit, in the metallic sun on the charcoaled pavement."

"Let me cut in a piece and stick on the moustache of the Nazi dictator who crushed Milena's tears and I heard her cries with my ethereal ears, hence after I was forbidden to die. I heard because, like God, the concentration camp of Auschwitz was also deaf."

"Have you tried to cry since that?" I asked

"No, never, you know–because my father has stolen my tears."

Marble Balls

The street urchins were ragged, not
tiny legged, but too long were their
femurs for fences; plucking down
plums with an unending bamboo stick,
perhaps for *prasad*, as the next day was
festive of supreme God Shiva's marriage;
going to be celebrated by dirty scaly tiny
hands; got trembled in the harrowing
harangue of the watchkeeper.
I saw from the balcony of a skyscraper.
They were looking like pebbles beside
the crescent moon, dropped down
from Lord Shiva's head but my God
was quite ignorant of it. He was in the
tiny shape of a podgy child, busy playing *kancha*.
I am still hearing the hitting sound of rolling marble balls.

Coagulated City

I still remember the dark hotel of an urban ship floated without water and I fumbled there in the dark mode to get myself to leap up the sordid heaplachases. An evening strolling with engulfing tea in earthen cups! The coal *chulha* was oozing black clouds and ice was in the air atoms.

All was there except my mother and the sooty fragrance. I left the stall twenty years back, though coal was still burning in which mother cooked flattened bread. I used to keep a sheepishly tiny batter of dough in the *chulha*. Tiny dinner was the real treasure of my father. A symbiotic bliss!

One day I was returning from the office in black car and a multiple-eyed old woman beckoned, making me stop. Relics of the village peeped out from crevices of the coagulated city and a big hotel was in the same place as the tea stall.

I dined there again along with my dear ones, though the chairs were vacant.

The Democratic Dungeon

I still like to sip coffee beneath an *Amaltas* tree, where frills of flesh linger beneath leaves because it is a tree of golden showers. I had a dog of butter, called Bulfer, buried under the *Amaltas*. Sipping coffee in buttery flavour drags my hypnagogia a hundred, hundred years back. I was driving Bulfer in the centre and it shifted to the left as soaring pus drooled in my right hemisphere. I tried to drain it, but Bulfer ran in as my right cerebrum began to whip. I live in a segment because my ancient emperors live now in a castle of ballots. I shift in my cell from time to time– right, left and centre–because I am a soulless bird of a democratic dungeon. I choose my cell by a ballot paper.

Grooming whiskers of Lincoln are metamorphosed into barren weeds!

The Green Pond

People talk about the green pond on the wayside road, on the bank of which I use to make childish chortles. Nowadays they are looking much greener. They ask me why I sit daily gazing upon green water?

My eyesight improves in a green glance, like my taste buds sharpen in chicken broth and my spectacle power has plummeted down. Nowadays I can see faraway with nude eyes. I dredged my filthy beats time and again, foiling my fossil heart, to get them drowned in the pond, but fortunately they survived upon the surface, to my agony and amazement.

Pink beats are swimmers, floating mosses now! Scum is spongy, scum is green. Gaping and gazing at my leftover bliss has made me also spongy.

Fractured God

Evening was soaked in sheets of solid rain. I saw a long flapping tail of a spotted dove on the parapet. Two tiny merl were slipping down in shrill sound, a fleshy girl was loitering with a thudding gait on the roof. My mother always tells me slim girls are easily selected as brides. A thick, fat, bundle of cash and a thin, fatless figure makes a perfect twinning of the groom and bride.

I would have collected all broken fingers in my fist, effacing the bar, but a boat-like tear erected in the air you were sitting in, mangled by memory of mine! Warm waves upon my electric flesh began to rejuvenate you again in the blissful beam.

I see a fractured God.

Helium Balloon

Pale pages of Das Kapital are wrapped in dust. A herdsman came, dusted off.

A biting termite emerged in big words and the moustache of Karl Marx began to grow in its wings. Helium Balloons swung up and up, punctured in iron bars.

Freedy Desmuth sulked, and died in a legitimacy war.

City Of Old Days

I am a wayfarer of long days, though I have many twisting knots in my stepping gait, making it in a meandering way. I have in my elbow a hanging sac. Like a punch bag, it has many marks of fists, bullets, missiles, but still it is there, trauma is to my elbow ligaments which have clumps of tears. Each year a new year and now to my nightmare there is a big hole. This sac is old enough to be tattered but refuses to leave me. At a mountain I saw a soldier with one eye, with a looping horn on his forehead, and I tried to bargain but horns began to drop piece by piece in my sac. That was enough for my ligaments and holes began to engulf shells, drones, arrows, knives, stones and bullets.

At a scintillating seashore I detoured for a while; too much for my eyes as I saw an angelic flash glittering in all four corners. He was Alan Kurdi, with shoes in a lapping wave. I tried to pull his wet shoes, and at once he sat up and gave me petunia flowers.

"Just go to the cross bridge where drones are descending and sell these flowers."

Look! The city of old days never dies, they will rejuvenate again and again in my little breath.

Note: Alan Kurdi (born as Aylan Shenu), initially reported as Aylan Kurdi, was a three-year-old Syrian boy of Kurdish ethnic background, whose image made global headlines after he drowned on 2 September 2015 in the Mediterranean Sea. He and his family were Syrian refugees trying to reach Europe amid the European refugee crisis.

Starfish

I want to tell a story of a ledge that erupted in the skull sky when the mellifluous moon was shriveled. Whole seas began to downpour on its edge and millions of bursting atoms squirted out. I am an extension of myself in a starfish, sea salt gushing through its pore. Starfish are feeders of the sea.

Whenever you come to me, a spoonful of salt mingles in this starfish soul of mine. The same sea skull begins to make noise tearing away its essence of equanimity.

Today, in the early morning, I see two starfish dancing in the sea whims. Their sprouting arms are in motion, soon my oars are going to kiss the seashore.

Coins

I looked around.

He came after a stale wait, chewing betel leaves. "Look, your paper is not authentic, many objections could be made by high authority. So many holes."

I dropped coins in the holes.

He stared, and his twitching cheek muscles suddenly started to wrestle to hold the red saliva.
"Don't lose heart, I will be always there for you."

A puff of wind swayed me and now I was at the exit door.

The Sentinel at the door returned my coins. Your old coins don't fit in holes now. You should have filled them up in holes in their running time."

Riot

I am sitting in the most corner, one chair beneath the last lamppost. Blind alley is black, prevailing in my eyelashes. It has been ten days since the newspaper came. Owls are sipping cold coffee. Cold is not waiting, but coldness is brewing in it. I want to unlock it in my mind. My apprehension is pale and blood is red.

Twilight is in the background and layers are in lines: apprehensive pale lines distilled in red lines, one saffron line invented. Sky is white and the clouds in the corners are blue.

I sought saffron as an emblem of sacrifice and enlightenment and tried to wash out my apprehensive blood. But, to my wonder, the brook took a sudden twist, went afar. Bricks of butterflies which were stagnant in the air, began to tumble in clusters from the corner of my roof. Elder family members had collected them as weapons, to throw upon the bigots. Bigotry is an interchangeable word for both blamers.

Suddenly, I felt sulking, and expurgated myself.

Newspapers have arrived now, a collection of butterflies are slain. I am looking at my ajar door.

Wine In The Coconut Shell

"Beauties are scattered in nude form on the sea beaches," Albert Camus whispered in a mesmerising moment. I agree with you, Albert.

One day, I was sipping wine by hiding it in a coconut shell. You were lingering in my memory. I seek salvation in hiding because I am a tropical lady. For centuary I didn't see the sun, though it was overhead, and I was in my anthill. I am a black ant trailing among stalagmites, skyscrapers and scruples in biting bread.

One day, I left my ant prints which were carved hundreds of years ago. I derailed and came beneath the same car of your last riding.

I still look for beaches and want to take a dip, but I cannot. You know my wings have gone along with you.

Dungeon

Reels of relocked rectangular files are in a vertical stand of a sepulchral library and termites are going on in a timeless streamline in the dungeon of dark letters. Government is their favourite niche!

I saw an outline of a thin blue cap over a pupa on a pile of pale pages which never metamorphosed. I tried to scan it and, to my irony, it was my father's signature. A signature speaks to the soul! It vanished in the insect gut. My father was a government officer.

I like to sip cold coffee sitting on the equator, mocking the overhead sun. Two leopards are mellowing down in the foam of iced coffee dripping from my mug.

Olfaction

You have bitten off a wedge of my red tongue and a dig of thousand years—a time scale noted. Since then, a dumbfounded dummy has been filling up that trench, dropping down pebbles. Pebbles are my concrete dreams, with the kernel of my relic lips baked in the melting heat of a snowman.

I spread yellow mustard seeds on the roof, feeding pigeons and, as I returned after a hundred years, my grandson welcomed me, though the mustard seeds were getting black. They were uneaten and beside them bark like plumage was sleeping. Gully boys giggle when they tie up cracker bombards in the tail of a fleeting dog.

That canine is captive in my olfactions and my receptors are bursting with dark swells.

The Black Soul

My ivory iris was bleached in the equatorial sun of my bedroom. I am looking for revelation through my ajar door. The black soul is tossing on the ethereal atoms of my courtyard, scampering in a jolt that descended beneath the rolling pin of my mother's kitchen. My mother serves me a circular chapati (bread) on the dining table. Like a painting by Salvador Dali, a book transforming into a nude woman, I saw a transformation of the four-dimensional into three dimensions. I began to eat bits of chapati, reducing myself to a tiny tot of yesteryears. My one auricle receives the *ajan* of mosque, twining with the chime of the splendorous temple of ancient Somnath in the next auricle. I feel myself moving like an ant in a church aisle.

I am standing in front of a cross. My white wagonette has arrived now.

Balzac's Black Coffee

In a tiny trance one day, I put my books in my rustic muddy stove along with dry wood. They smoked up in the sky through a puffing chimney. Books are now in the sky, in the white fog hoofing down by the stallions, columned in my country for centuries.

Beneath is a derelict, charred, half-burnt library. I squirted water to break the lockdown of flames. Soon they cooled and a big volume of "The Human Comedy" peeped out. As I touched, the bulk of the grounds of Robusta coffee began to bicker on the floor. They were out of the clutch of old invaders, secured in lockdown! Roasted entrails of Balzac were stuck in the index. I tried to remove the sticky one but— redundant! Perhaps Balzac had left it in oblivion.

The coffee-fuelled pen of Balzac still sips black coffee and foams out espresso.

Whenever I sip, Balzac's Paris beams in the bottom of my mug!

Golden Bird

I took shelter in the farthest east, swam across the oceans, squirting water under my fluttering wings. I knew my destination. It has been rhymed in folklore chants and songs of gods. I descended there and sipped diamond drops in an ethereal brook. My fabric changed: I was now a golden bird. It was the magic of elixir or the effect of hypnosis on demigods. I leave it upon your boundless imagination. I became a golden bird. My gleam stole away the twilight. Words of distant Avesta resounded and echoed in four vedas. Light of Asia emerged in my halted and rather native land. The sparkling serenity swayed around, music of heaven's bliss descended in every pebble, lush leaves and dews. Such was the effect of land of Charle's wain. Everything was nice unless even kings and warriors laid down their swords. Magic of limpid spirituality, their swords stole away in washing and cleaning their souls. Swords heaped up in dirt and rotted in rusted fossils. My doomsday paved away as invaders' hoofs began to downpour in sheets and columns. I plummeted down, my wing clipped away. I drank red drops and thought, "Why did the warrior sip ethereal drops?"

Coins Of Corona

The parturient land and wrinkled hand smeared in sweat, takes one year to make mounds of lentils, veggies, rice and wheat. The democratic demons engulf it all in one mere gulp, basking in glory of an eagle emperor. The food given to medic servants shrivels in one fist, though they are in mountains on government paper. One day, I saw a murder of crows appointed as admins in this dungeon, because they had developed eerie entrails with a silencer!

I read in the biology book that crows swallow without chewing, but crows of my country belch in a magical wand, so they don't even make a sound.

Nowadays their nests are teeming with corona coins.

Footnote: Nowadays doctors are dying, administrators are relishing as so many plans are on paper in the name of corona, and leaders are busy in their election.

Bleeding Star

The sheep which was toothless has suddenly started grazing on the meadow slopes of the hills. He was dipped in the red sea long ago and has finally found his recurring destiny.

Graze, graze, graze!

And that destiny is stale, like the leftover bread from the rolling board of my grandmother. But the most astonishing thing happened when I came to collect the stars which had been bleeding for millions of years. Only my mother had seen them and she weaved them into the story for me to bargain her teats whenever I used to refuse to suck them.

Bleeding stars have never left me. My medic eyes caught the tiny tot who was bleeding in a big pool and began to submerge. I tried to pull him by the hair but the fiery wavelets crafted on his scalp. Medical books tag them: "Hair-on end appearance."

Fasting Farmers In The Supermarket

The Fermenting fearsome farmers are fasting beneath salty sun and postcolonial parliament talks in defiance. The bill is fluttering in pupa, and pupa in the cocoon, and I am peeling its layers to pull it free; but soiled, wrinkled hands drag me as they call it a capitalist concoction. I know Yeats of Sligo is still counting blood drops to draw his scalpel on right and wrong. I am friendlier to him because I like to dip the full moon in Ganga and draw its black digs with black sketches before getting stuck in the pile of black carpet. I am among farmers of India, though the Irish famine is not alien to me and also dried flesh. I ate potatoes to fill my empty stomach and I like the beard of Sean Connery. I began to love Scotland after visiting "Braveheart" in the movie hall of the supermarket. Mel Gibson was marvellous! All are wrapped in a single aura and I punctured it to get a hybrid. I like to swallow the tail fins of fish as they are stuck on both flesh and spinal cord. But Mediterranean fish is fleshy and I think Albert Camus would wash it down with wine.

Part 3

My Father's Tunic

The tunic of my father is still on the tenterhooks, though alienated in aura as dust is in the air.

One day I saw it nibble out in multiple holes. My mother sewed it for a hundred years.

My wrinkled eyes are now in arcus senilis and, in a vast vacuum, I am sucking the teats of my mother!

Alienated Laugh

I squeezed a pinch of my flesh, my filtered laugh leaking in a long trail. I chopped it with a red flower and kept it on the toy train. My daughter chortles in countless choruses when the train whistles in a giggle. In a frisky, frenzy she pushes it.

I am sitting in my mother's lap. I plucked a mummified moon from out of the bangles of witches who used to stalk in the night: too much for my goose bumps!

I see my alienated laugh on the train.

Scandal

N is just sipping coffee, though it stopped in a start as each sip brought ballooning of charred cheeks.

Cheeks are swollen now!

His mouth opens in a hole, or in the line of a tubular vision. He just rises early and sits, as it seems his eye has been caught in the notes of the puffed piano. The whole music is locked and waiting for the French Revolution which will bring bread to belching borrowers .

Until then, eat Cake !

One day, as he was in search of a voyage, like Columbus, though his routine was set like a cylinder in the kitchen after children are escorted to school, he discovered that his major work had been done. He slipped in the mud of stagnant squelch. Two wolves were at the ends of the rope. They began to circle round and round and suddenly N noted multiple mounds upon his body. A big one was pushing out of his skull, tasseled like a bickering soul.

A bump in the soul!

A tattered soul weakens one and is a feast for wolves! One day, as usual, he was sipping coffee, when a big booming wave of the whole sea began to overflow in the cup. A mermaid sipped the coffee in his mouth, an ocean of outlandish elixir flowing in his heart.

Sometimes scandals are concocted by God.

A rescue!

Inkwell

My neighbour puffs costly Cohiba cigars in the nicotine of Nietzsche and bargains with a dark, viscous vendor upon the tiny bundle of spinach for one hour. Kafka's magical realism sways and swings in the soiled hands of filthy farmers: grains, potatoes, green chillies, and veggies of mere crusted coins are dancing in dollars in big malls.

A big shepherd was drinking red wine and untwirled the key. Flocks of sheep began to trail in teeming trance, terminated in the red sea.

One day I will slay the one who is hiding in me and then throw them in my inkwell.

Coffer Box

I lifted up the lid of my coffee-colored coffer box, laid in limitless time, which suddenly began to whimper and melt. They liquefied in the wide sea. I would have sipped them, but just waited and scanned them carefully, one by one. Pale presence of talks, white talks, tawdry talks, mauve talks, red talks ... of every hue I had ever imagined. Suddenly, the thawness of liquid vanished like a bodied one. It reminded me that, once upon a time, they shook the world.

Brief bit of reincarnation!

I took them one by one and threw them in the ethereal sea. They gleamed like serene sacred sonnets. I gaped for a while, gave a detached look. Infinite peace descended upon me.

I belong to all, all belongs to me.

My stoic soul sold my every fibre and flesh and I sang "Songs of Electric," leaning upon a pyre.

Sharer

My Father brought two apples. One for himself, one for mother.
"One for sun and one for moon."

We siblings were lyricists of leisure time which we sought in moonlight. In the night, the share market plummeted! The sun's apple was slithering under the burden of holders. We clung to the bankrupt moon!

My mother apple is still running in the moneyed world.

Bereavement

I saw with my rainy eyes the snoozing guard in the pigsty beneath the lamppost. Goosebumps in chilled drops of rain turned into wrinkles when they heard about your departure, as the void of absence was alive in the pale presence of sunlight. Bereavement beneath the bawdy sun broke the axle of my soul with a loud sound, though my deafened ear perceived the merest faint chime of the temple. Sooner or later, I will wave my silver spoon, studded with gems, which will catch the black digs of the moon which have gone before you.

And I am beneath the void sky of a full moon.

Though you didn't write to me, written words are whimpering at my window sill. One day, I will swallow them, hold them in my breast. It's all are matter of moment.

Sweetheart, you have gone long before.

My Father's Wristwatch

A white wristwatch was left alive in my father's ash urn. I wrapped it in my tiny hand. I grew up , and the watch also grew rounded, plumped into a wall clock. Nowadays it hangs on the wall beside my father's portrait.

I am stuck for a minute, moving around.

One day, two shooting stars dropped upon it, and the wall clock fell down on the floor. My tiny wrist broke down in a mangled minute hand. My mother told me not to try to fix it, or my fingers would also break.

The hour hand has circled a thousand times round, though my minutes are stagnant still. My mother lives in my broken minute hand.

I am still trying to fix it with my mother's knife.

Incarnation

A small vial has sat on the altar of my home for thousands of years. Drop by drop, my ancestors sipped, as Ganga gurgled to heaven.

One day I emptied it in my mouth.

I see the torso of a man stuck on the lower half of a fish, swimming in my room. A surge of flood water saturates my bed.

Incarnation of lord Vishnu occurs in a tiny vial!

Mother's Postcard

The postcard was blank as words were eaten by the new moon. Today was Amavasya! I would have located the address, rolling in the virtual rings of ethereal atoms, but stony Sisyphus came to rest beneath the bawdy sun and his shoulders were bruised in a trailing salty brook.

"Keep this one for a brief time."

I took the gravitating stone on my chest. Dark was so compressed that all twitterers were shut in the twilight and I awoke in my wrinkles. It was neither dream nor hypnagogia, too much for my crushed chest. I saw the words on the pale postcard.

"She died last night."

I Am Covid Positive

The dark hole was pale in self-isolation and my virtual world was banished inside a virus cube. Nowadays, I live there and, yes, I sometimes rove my eyes left and right, as vitreous fluid becomes stagnant in muddy irises. Night descends upon curved eyelids and I have for one month seen stars scuttering like skylarks here.

You know I am insomniac now and so I am a watcher in the playground. Being an audience to oneself makes a blue prism, a cold castle, though I am still pink there, as autumn is my favorite. My fragile fingers stop between platter and mouth as they tuck in tremor. I am hungry now, though my fridge is stuffed.

One day it happened: two stars were clogged in my dark hole and I saw a shriveled woman sitting in one dimension, her face wrapped in a pestle-white towel.

Virus slept on my medic palms and I am covid positive now.

I Locked The Lake

Ten owls are flocking in heaven. In a demon's trance they engulf the colour of night. Black owls are fluttering in white night!

A frail, tepid cry formed a vertical column, up and up in the pale air, near the horizontal flesh of my father. I was twirling in thunder between two blocks. My mother was stumbling at night along a collection of breaths. All except one. Sojourn was going to the bank for a brief time as water overflowed. I simply collected all the tears and it all rose like a freshet.

I locked the lake.